Rattles, the Barn Cat Misfit

Arlene White

Written and Illustrated by
Arlene White

D1313667

Copyright ©2007-2017 by Arlene Sevilla-White
ISBN: Softcover   9781549905391

All rights reserved. No part of this book may be reproduced
or transmitted in any form or by any means, electronic or mechanical,
including photocopying, recording, or
by any information storage and retrieval system, without
permission in writing from the copyright owner.

This is a work of fiction. Names, charcters, places and
incidents either are the product of the author's imagination
or are used fictitiously, and any resemblance to any actual
persons, living or dead, events, or locales is
coincidental.

Acknowledgements

This book is dedicated to my mom, who has now passed. She was an inspiration for a key character in the book, and her memory will forever be in my heart.

A special thanks to my husband, Scott, my daughters, Linda and Michelle, my brother, Duane, and my friend, Arnoldo, for all their love and support.

Also a special thanks to my friend, Jane Reiter, for helping me to edit the book.

Rattles was a barn cat. She lived in a haymow with her two sisters, one brother, and her mother. There were lots of other cats that lived there, too. Many of them were her cousins and her aunts and uncles. All of the cats in the haymow were wild. All of them except Rattles, that is. **Rattles was different.**

There weren't many people that lived on the farm – only Grandma and Uncle Duane. Grandma and Uncle Duane did not play with the cats, so the cats were afraid of humans. All of them except Rattles, that is. **Rattles was different.**

Rattles loved humans. When Uncle Duane milked the cows, Rattles would jump onto his lap. When Grandma fed the calves, Rattles would follow her. And when Grandma went for a walk, Rattles would jump on her shoulder, ride along, and purr a purr so big she sounded like a rattle. ***Rattles was different.***

One day two children arrived on the farm. Their names were Linda and Michelle, and they had come to visit Grandma. *"Kitties!"* shouted Linda as she crawled out of the van. *"Grandma, do you have any new baby kittens?"*

"I sure do," smiled Grandma. *"There's a litter of four kittens in the haymow. They're all wild though – all of them except one that is."* That one was Rattles, of course. **Rattles was different.**

4

Linda and Michelle shouted with excitement. They loved cats. Linda ran to the barn, crawled up the ladder to the haymow, and immediately began to look for kittens.

All the cats began to run. Rattles' two sisters ran, her brother ran, and her mother ran. All of her aunts, uncles, and cousins ran. All of her friends ran. *"Danger,"* they all hissed. *"There's a human here."* They all crawled into some holes between the straw bales to hide – all of them except Rattles that is. **Rattles was different.**

5

"I like humans," purred Rattles with a rattling purr that was so loud her whole body shook. *"Humans are nice. Why this human is a child like me! I bet she would be fun to play with."* Rattles put her tail straight up in the air, waddled over to Linda, and purred some more.

"Kitty!" yelled Linda as she picked up Rattles. Linda held Rattles close to her body as she carried her down the ladder and to Grandma's house. Rattles wasn't afraid. **Rattles was different.**

Michelle greeted Linda and Rattles at the door. *"Let me hold her! Let me hold her!"* she cried. Linda let Michelle take the cat. Rattles again shook with her rattling purr. *"This cat's name must be Rattles,"* said Michelle. *"Her purr sounds like a rattle. . . Mom! Dad! Listen to Rattles purr!"*

Linda, Michelle, and their mom and dad stayed at Grandma's house for three days. Every morning they would bring Rattles to the house and play with her all day. Every night they would bring Rattles to the haymow so she could be back with her family. There was an uproar in the cat community during the nights. *"Rattles,"* the other cats warned. *"You can't trust humans! You have to run when the children come. They're dangerous."*

But Rattles would only reply, *"They're not dangerous. They're fun and they're nice. They play string with me. They dress me in doll clothes. They feed me milk."* Rattles wasn't afraid. **Rattles was different.**

On the fourth morning, though, when Linda went to visit Rattles in the haymow, she had tears in her eyes.
"Rattles," she said, *"today we have to go back home to the city. I will take you to Michelle for a few minutes so we can say good-bye."*

When Michelle saw Rattles, she cried, too. *"Rattles, I love you. I wish you could come to the city with us."* Rattles was sad. She wished she could come, too. She didn't know what it was like in the city, but she didn't want to be like the other barn cats. ***Rattles was different.***

It just wasn't the same for Rattles after the girls left. She missed Linda and Michelle. She missed playing string with them. She missed having them put those funny, little doll clothes on her. But most of all she missed all the attention that they gave to her. She felt – well, she felt….special. That was it….She felt special around them. Oh sure, Rattles played with the other cats, but they were dull by comparison. **They were different.**

Rattles was sad. *"Rattles… Rattles. Come on Rattles. Cheer up. Let's play run through the straw bales,"* said one of her sisters. But Rattles shook her head no. *"Boring,"* she thought to herself.

*"**R**attles… Rattles. Let's play hiss and spit at each other,"* said another one of her sisters.

"No.. no, thank you." said Rattles. *"It's stupid,"* she thought to herself.

"Oh, R…a…t…t…l…e…s. Let's play stare at the dog," said one of her friends.

"No, that's okay," said Rattles. Rattles shook her head, and thought to herself, ***"They sure are different!"***

The days started getting colder, and Rattles was getting sick. Her nose was runny. Her eyes were runny. Her stomach hurt. Rattles felt miserable.

Grandma even noticed. *"Oh, dear,"* said Grandma. *"The girls will be upset if something happens to Rattles."* Grandma picked up Rattles and carried her to the car. *"Rattles, I'm afraid we're going to have to take you to the vet."*

When Grandma returned home from the veterinary, she kept Rattles in the house to keep her warm and had some special medicine to give her with an eye dropper. Rattles could hardly swallow it.

Rattles was only in the house for two days when she heard some familiar voices… *"Happy Thanksgiving, Grandma!.... Rattles! You're here. You look sick!"*

It was Linda and Michelle! Rattles tried to purr, but her throat was too sore.

The girls were again having a three-day stay at Grandma's. They played with Rattles a lot, but they let her rest a lot, too.

They were ready to go back to the city on the fourth morning when disaster struck. Rattles' brother was badly hurt by the farm dog. The humans tried to help him, but when Uncle Duane tried to catch him, he would only hide. Everyone could only hope for the best.

"Mom! Dad!" the girls cried. *"Can Rattles please come home with us? Please? We don't want her to get hurt by the farm dog, too."*

"But we have a puppy at home," replied Dad.

"Our puppy is friendly and gentle, though. Please?!"

"Well… okay," replied Dad.

Grandma packed Rattles' medicine and the box she had
been sleeping in while in the house. Everyone piled into the
van. Rattles got to sit in the front seat on Mom's lap.

It was the longest ride Rattles ever had. They rode and rode
and rode. One hour – two hours – three hours – four hours.
"I don't know," thought Rattles to herself. *"This is really long
and boring for a sick cat."*

23

But things changed after five hours. Suddenly there were bright lights shining all over in the dark. There were more buildings than Rattles could ever have imagined. And cars – there were cars - so many cars they looked almost piled up on top of one another. Rattles sat at attention watching out the window. This was exciting! *Now this was different.*

Rattles knew she was almost at her new home when the family stopped at someone's house to pick up the family's playful, friendly puppy. They then went to a grocery store to get some cat food.

When the van stopped again in another driveway, Rattles knew she was at her new home and started to purr. She could hardly wait to investigate the inside of the pretty, red-brick house. Yes – it sure was going to be different in the city, but then **Rattles was different, too!**

ABOUT THE AUTHOR
Arlene White

www.ArleneWhite.com

Arlene White's passions started as a kid - writing, art and animals. She grew up on a dairy farm around a lot of barn cats and animals, so loving cats and animals was a given. Her passion for art developed as she watched her mom do crafts, and as she took English classes in school, she discovered writing was a natural.

As an adult, Arlene White started working in business, later became an elementary-school art teacher, and now devotes her time to writing and illustrating children's books. Her inspiration for the series, "Rattles, the Barn Cat," came from her family's farm.

Get your FREE audiobook of the first book in this series at:

www.ArleneWhite.com/free-audiobook

Rattles merchandise is also available at:

www.ArleneWhite.com

18091872R00019

Made in the USA
Lexington, KY
20 November 2018